Rex vs. Wheeler

Dov Needleman

Rex vs. Wheeler

By Dov Needleman

Copyright 2021 Dov Needleman

KDP Print Edition

Dedicated to those who fight with a muted voice.

For my loved ones.

Imagination takes no orders, nor prisoners...

n a flash, Wheeler zooms his way across a busy Hollywood intersection. He's traveling so fast that oncoming traffic has no time to break. Whizzing past two lanes of cars, time slows as tires screech towards him. He bends low to the ground, leaping up in late afternoon, kick-flipping his skateboard just high enough to graze the hood of a car, exhaling over the windshield. He lands the jump perfectly, sliding his wheels to a cutting horizontal stop just before hitting the graffitied wall of a tall building. Those that catch a glimpse of the action hoot and holler after him in awe and disapproval. He leaves those trying to approach him in a cloud of dust, kicking to the asphalt accelerating behind him.

Slithering along a sidewalk on Hollywood Blvd, some kids riding bikes and skateboards recognize Wheeler. Shouting with delight, they hurry to catch up with him. He slows his roll, smiling and laughing, as they swirl in circles around him. At the corner of the next intersection, Wheeler looks up ahead to a cluster of tall buildings. Many of the building walls have advertisements for upcoming concerts and feature films lighting up the way for those walking the streets below. One ad stands out from all the rest, catching his eye. He glances up at brightness shining off a mega display screen promoting one of the city's most celebrated events, Skate Masters. The commercial shows skate footage from this year's contenders. Many of the clips are taken from prior Skate Masters events. Of all the skaters depicted, most of the screen time belongs to Wheeler and Rex. The final scene boasts, "Rex vs. Wheeler," in striking neon design, with images of their heads faced inwardly towards the highlighted words.

Skate Masters is a world-renowned club that pursues the most talented skaters from all parts of the globe. The club hosts multiple qualifying tournaments throughout the year. Winners of these tournaments have a chance to attend exclusive skate retreats. A semi-annual retreat takes place in a new and undisclosed location by special invitation. Only by attending a retreat will a skater have the opportunity to be voted into the Skate Masters premier event held in Venice Beach every two years. For the upcoming one, all eyes rest on Rex or Wheeler to win the big air event.

The skate culture in Los Angeles remains stronger than ever. By nature, skaters explore all of the unique terrain the concrete jungle has to offer. It's a special time for local skaters because Rex and Wheeler are from around the corner. In the small town of Santa Monica, both discover their passions for skateboarding. Although they grow up within a few blocks of each other, Wheeler comes from a wealthy household and Rex without a house at all.

Wheeler has lived all his life in a beachfront estate with his family. He becomes addicted to extreme sports from the moment he can balance on a board. He has a team of elite trainers, cutting-edge equipment and access to the best remote skate spots. He wins his first Skate Masters qualifying tournament at the age of twelve, and by his dedication to all that he learns in years of training and attending retreats, at fifteen he is voted into his first Skate Masters event, subsequently winning three straight premier events; unable to win a fourth, being banned from flying from his ski base in Switzerland due to a "blizzard."

    Outside the gates of Wheeler's beach mansion, Rex skates by slowly. He stares blankly at the sprawling estate, shrugging to himself as the property vanishes from his sight. Kicking hard to the ground, he bounds forward, picking up speed. Light reflecting off the monstrous homes beside him splash upon the smooth black road, streaking past him. Skidding around the bend to a place beyond a narrow alleyway between the street and sandy beach, he notices a group of bicyclists huddling on the corner of an intersection giving him looks of uncertainty and murmuring to each other. He rolls his eyes, riding along to the rhythm of his rolling wheels until reaching the ideal skate spot, an important piece to the puzzle of places comprising his makeshift home growing up. Located in a secluded area off the beaten path of tourism, concealing the perfect amount of space, full of obstacles, slopes and stairs, beckoning the initiated few who know the place.

    Rex stands on the edge, imagining each speck of park terrain that his wheels have skated past in days of freedom spent there. Tiring rays melt into chalky slopes like drips of sorbet. He swoons through on his skateboard, circling the area, keeping a respectful distance from those around. Some of the skaters nudge each other, pointing discretely towards him. Picking up momentum on the slopes, hopping stair gaps and switching up his grind style mid-rail, his talent is obvious. The air seems to vacuum for those watching nearby, breathlessly staring, mesmerized by the spectacle.

Sunshine descends upon the treasured place. Remnants of light remain suspended within the muraled walls of adjacent buildings where Rex resides in a penthouse. It's a massive flat with floor to ceiling glass walls and ocean views leaning over the horizon. He purchased the elaborate pad after winning the last Skate Masters event two years ago while Wheeler remained stuck in Switzerland. Both are set to compete in the imminent Skate Masters event which many believe will be the skate competition for the ages.

Rex is one year old when his mother disappears. His father was never in the picture. In a downtrodden, drug-infested apartment, the neighbors find Rex alone in his mother's bed. They make an anonymous call to the police after rummaging the place for anything of value. The door to the abandoned apartment is left wide open when police come in to find Rex laying quietly on a bare mattress shoved into a corner of the room. He is placed under government care and shuffled between an assortment of orphan homes. These homes become a fading memory, trailing a path over the horizon of his mind, faintly disappearing as he would run far away from each one.

Rex is seven years old in Southern California, living in another place he will never call "home." His foster mom sits in the kitchen, hardly present in a dead-end dream. The only color in her skin from bruising. She stares into the void of light reflecting off the white refrigerator door reciting scripture to the instrument of rosary beads trickling through her crippled fingertips. His foster dad barges into a room where Rex is sitting alone and scared. The man is drunk and his pants are wrapped around his ankles. He has intentions of abusing Rex, even if Rex does cooperate with his intoxicated commands. The incoherent fool suddenly breaks the beer bottle in his hand, pointing the dripping edges at Rex from the door. Glaring at the man, feeling entrapped, Rex desperately bolts to the shut window in the room. He leaps out, shattering the glass and tumbling onto the dying front lawn. Blood oozes from the corner of his eyebrow and his arms and legs are sliced up. The foster monster rams the front door and rips through the screen. He staggers belligerently towards the boy while attempting to pull up his pants. Rex runs to the end of the driveway where a teenager is skateboarding along the sidewalk. Bursting at the skater, knocking him hard to the ground with a lowered propelling shoulder, he hops on the escaping board and hits hard to the ground. Disappearing down the street, having never ridden before, he skates all through the night.

It's only three days before the Skate Masters event and commotion from the nearing festivities has brought skaters from all over the world to Los Angeles. Many streets are roped off for swarms of those on wheels to roam freely in Venice Beach. Rex makes his way over to Venice from the treasured skate spot in Santa Monica to immerse himself in some of the action. Donning a baseball cap with sunglasses covering much of his face to avoid being seen, he makes his way through the crowds. Reaching one of the many skate bowls around, he sits, skateboard in lap and feet dangling. He focuses on the periodic waves gracefully pulsing to shore. The sunset burns through the horizon line, melting the sky with warm desert colors that dance about the smoking clouds like splatters of clay paint. The air is thin, an imperceptible atmosphere, except for the most subtle breeze that comes and goes with the whispering tide.

Rex closes his eyes, inhaling the salty air until his lungs are totally expanded, then softly releases his breath. Turning his attention back to the skate bowl, encouraging cheers are heard from rows of people watching from behind the rails. As he looks around, his wandering gaze suddenly fixates upon the most beautiful young woman he has ever seen. His stomach drops before he has a chance to gulp, coughing out loud. Wiping his eyes with the bottoms of his palms, trying hard not to stare, he's entranced by streaks of light bouncing delicately off her long free-falling hair. Before he knows it, he's back on his board, gliding down the chalky surface of the skate bowl. Accelerating effortlessly, all eyes fall upon him. Ripping up and down the steep inclines, gaining momentum, he dings his wheels lightly on the curving rail, backflipping at the pace of a tired dream above the heads of those watching within the bowl's peninsula, perfectly hitting the landing. Caroming upwards on the opposite end, grinding backside along the edge of the rail, sparks spewing off his wheels, he drops back in, heel-flipping in free fall, screeching to a stop at the bowl's nadir. Those watching from behind the rails cheer in appreciation, swarming along the edges. He takes a friendly bow, acknowledging the applause. The beautiful young woman peers down with the others. She and Rex find each other, smiling irresistibly, their eyes flaring up. She turns to walk back through the crowd, her departing figure disperses into the chaos of people surrounding them.

A boy appears from around a curve of the skate bowl, riding fast along its sloping interior. Unaware of Rex's presence, he crashes into Rex's heel with the lip of his skateboard, bouncing off Rex's back, falling hard to the ground. Rex shouts out in pain, viciously pivoting towards the boy. Realizing the angry expression on Rex's face, the boy quickly gathers his skateboard, running up the bowl's slope, pushing through the crowd and hurt to the bone. Witnesses to the accident disappointedly thin out from the onlooking circle around the bowl. Rex drops his head with a sense of regret, plopping down to sit forlorn on his board. He twirls the hairs on his head until a hiccup of repressed air releases him from a reel of anxious thoughts. Looking up slowly, he sees those that were goggling down on him have moved on.

Rex jumps upright, climbing his way out of the skate bowl, setting off in the direction of the boy he mistreated. He directs his sight to the winding pathways along the beach, searching faces passing by.

After covering a couple of blocks, just when he is about to give up, he sees the boy sitting on a curb in an empty lot. The boy's feet slowly swing back and forth like a pendulum with his skateboard, his head hanging gloomily in crossed arms. Rex comes to an abrupt stop in front of the boy, who perks up his head. He stares confusedly at Rex with lines of stained tears down his face and a fresh tear just below his left eye. Rex sits down next to him. Looking out at it all, performing clever tricks with his skateboard. The boy's expression changes, smiling as he watches, wiping a tear from his face. Rex offers a handshake. The boy nods his head slowly with approval, shaking his hand. Rex notices the ragged nature of the boy's clothing and hygiene. The boy is sitting next to an open backpack containing a few articles of clothing and empty food wrappers. Rex walks across the street to a convenience store. Returning with pen and paper, he writes his name, address, and phone number. He grabs some cash from his wallet and takes the boy's hand, placing the note and money in his grasp. Rex turns away, skating off around the corner to the beachfront street, headed north in the direction of Santa Monica.

Riding along the sandy sidewalk, Rex grimaces in pain from his injured heel. He skids to a stop, noticing a building with no windows, a single door and a small fluorescent sign that reads, "Cocktails." He weighs his options, deciding that with only three days left before the Skate Masters event he should probably just go home, but he walks toward the fluorescent sign instead.

A large man in a skintight t-shirt at the door lets Rex in even though there is a line for the bar wrapped around the block. The music is blasting inside the dark, crowded room and it's challenging to make out the faces of pulsating bodies within. Only light from the single door opening and closing enables a brief period for self-orientation. The moment Rex enters the bar a young woman's deafening shriek catches him off guard. Without hesitation, she takes flight. Limbs spread, she wraps around him like a koala clinging to a tree. Rex half spins in both directions unable to comprehend the best way to remove her. She kisses his cheek three times and slides off him, skipping away into the mob of dancing bodies.

Rex turns his attention to the bar locking eyes with the bartender whose face reveals that he witnessed Rex be affectionately mauled. He waves Rex over, "First one's on the house." Rex picks up the glass of whiskey and takes a short sip. Licking his chops, he leers over at a young woman standing next to him. She has a disturbed look for him, cupping hand over cheek to block him from seeing her face before walking away in a hurry. Rex rips the rest of it, slamming the bar with his glass. He turns to look out at the sea of intoxicated adults wiggling on the dance floor.

Rex makes eye contact with a girl holding liquor bottles and sparklers above her head. She brightens up, nodding for him to follow her. He moves to catch her, weaving around the dancing bodies without making physical contact. She drops the bottles off at a table of partiers who demolish the liquor in a matter of moments. She grabs him by the hand, pulling him into the roped off VIP table section, then pours him a drink from a bottle on somebody else's table.

Before taking a sip, Rex locks eyes with a young woman who looks like something out of a fairy tale. His eyes follow her until she stops dead in her tracks, right as she is about to walk out the door with her friend. She stares at Rex with her dark purple eyes. He sits atop the back of a velvet couch in the VIP section, staring motionlessly back at her. She puts a finger up for her friend to wait, then walks back through the club towards him. Never breaking eye contact, within arm's reach, their stares turn to smiles from ear to ear. Without slowing her pace, without him flinching an inch, they connect. She pulls him towards her by his shirt. They French kiss for a few seconds before an interruption by the bottle girl handing them both drinks. The friend appears by her side to whisper something in her ear. She looks at Rex with her dark purple eyes and they lean in to kiss for a few more seconds. She puts out her hand and Rex gives her his phone. Putting her number in and handing it back, she pushes him playfully over the back of the couch. He topples over, losing grip of his phone and smashing into the bottles on another table. Rummaging around in the dark on the sticky floor, avoiding stomping feet, he locates his phone, stuffs it back in his pocket and crawls away from the confusion surrounding the smashed glass.

Rex sees a group of young men hanging out at a table on the opposite end of the VIP section in the far back corner. There are two imported velvet sofas facing inwardly with a table full of bottles in the middle. He stumbles into their drunken huddle and they erupt with shouts of excitement. Shots are poured as they yell and chant to the thumping music, properly topped off. They dance around aimlessly looking for women to come near.

Rex locks eyes with an exotic angel. She allures him, waltzing by his shoulder. They smile brightly at each other. Her friend appears and all three of them start dancing to the heavy bass blaring from the surround sound speakers. The group of guys, joined by more gals, all go wild. Grinding up on each other, lost, having the time of their lives. The two ladies Rex has his arms around start kissing each other and he pokes his face in between. They continue to sway with their faces beaming, staring into each other's eyes. The dazzling ladies fall into the sofa bringing Rex with them, regaining composure on his lap as they make out. Those nearby shine their phone cameras on the trio, dancing and laughing as they record the madness. Unaffected by the cameras, closing their eyes to the shine, the three of them giggle and party on. The ladies push Rex's face away, standing up on the sofa and bouncing above the heads of the rest. He sits in between them drinking, self-absorbed in a frazzle-haired daze. A bouncer forces his way through the mob, shining a flashlight on the sofa-conquering ladies, signaling for them to step down. Ignoring him, they flick him off and dance with even more unruliness. Two more bouncers arrive from the depths of the crowd, each throwing a lady over his shoulder. One of the ladies pounds her fists against the bouncer's back, ineffectively squirming to be put down as her friend grabs a drink out of someone's hand, chugs it and throws the empty glass back into the crowd. Finishing his drink, Rex watches the entire scenario play out as he stands on a sofa with the best view of it all.

Feeling detached from the energy, Rex wanders back through dancing bodies. Swinging open the single door with his head down, he walks a block before looking up at the clear midnight sky. He pulls out his phone, awestruck by the memory of the first young woman with purple eyes he met earlier that night. Texting to find out her location: a nearby bar. Wasting no time, he dashes off to meet her. Intoxicated and confident, he tries leaping over a curbed median in the street. Unable to clear the jump, his ankle rolls on impact. His fast reflexes prevent him from falling with further injury. He's able to stand up and sees that he can walk. Alcohol masking most of the pain, he remembers where he is headed. Smiling in appreciation of his own suffering, he makes way for the reward of a greater unknown.

Rex breezes into the place that's not jam-packed, still dark and blasting music with plenty of people wreaking havoc inside. Seeing her dancing by the bar with her friend, he approaches her. As soon as they make eye contact, both dart at each other's lips, kissing ferociously. The two of them grind slowly against each other, sipping through straws. More friends appear and they all party until the lights come on. The group stumbles onto the street, squeezing into a cab to head back to their elegant hotel which is bordered with ancient trees sprayed by the late night's vibrant moonlight. Swirling branches create illusionary shadows over the sprawling beachfront property. A crescent moon hovers nearby. Flooding light reflects off the ocean into the wide eyes of the group; nobody else around to witness the beauty of that place and time. An infinity shaped pool has entrances at its two flowery ends. Only steps from the sand, Rex sweeps her off her feet, jumping in. She falls over his body under water, reappearing at the end closest to the ocean. He swims over to be with her. They adjust to shallow depths of the pool, lounging comfortably. Friends smile at each other, waving temporary goodbyes to explore other parts of the hotel grounds in private. Straddling him, she giggles and waves them off. She and Rex have sex in the wading water while dusk turns to dawn at the rate of dreaming waves hugging to shore.

There is a jacuzzi molded to a stone wall with a cascading waterfall and bamboo showers located next to the pool. They explore each other's bodies in the rushing hot water of the stony shallow well until they're completely detoxified. He pulls her out of the steam and she walks over to talk with some of her friends. Rex jumps into the pool, enlivened from the shift to cooler temperature. He swims the distance of the pool's figure eight shape, emerging at the other end, within arm's reach of the sand, absorbing watercolor blots of early morning sky as calm waves submerge his mind in peace.

Rex emerges from the pool as she comes up to him, hugging him closely. She looks at him with her dark purple eyes and tells him in her exotic, slightly British accent, "I must return to my home in Thailand." They kiss a little longer before she turns her back on him. Rex watches her go, grabbing an untouched bottle of champagne resting in a steel-engraved bucket by their poolside cabana. He walks determinedly away, leaving a drippy trail of icy water behind with the hotel.

In a windowless octagonal studio with floor to ceiling mirrored walls, Wheeler stands on a white pine floor facing a trainer wearing boxing pads. He kicks his right foot up to meet the trainer's protected left hand. The kick echoes through the room. He follows with two kicks and a final spinning kick that smacks the pad off the trainer's hand. Wheeler and the trainer bow to each other. The trainer walks to retrieve the pad as Wheeler locates a keypad built into one of the walls. Entering a passcode, one mirror opens revealing a dark hallway.

Wheeler steps into a tunnel completely out of sight from the studio. His bare feet are cold on the sterile pathway. A series of dotted lights line the way leading to a door in the distance. He looks down at his feet to a security floor deciphering his footprints as he walks. His identity confirmed, the door ahead shines green, retracting in four directions from its middle. He continues onward as spirals of white light glow through the tunnel. He looks to his left to see an image of a jelly fish with smooth tentacles propelling along the tunnel wall. A computer-generated voice fills the air, "The current weather is 78°F, partly cloudy, the pickup point is 34° latitude -118° longitude," travels sweetly along with his walking pace. The jellyfish display is held up at the next secure door. As the door splits open, the jellyfish bobs up and down in place, "Don't forget to wear a helmet," echoes as the door tightly winks shut behind him.

Wheeler steps into a secure cabin. Dim strips of light illuminate the floorboards. The wall space is filled with extreme sports boards and various weapons. Blueprints are out on a table in the room's center, along with a notebook which he snags up. On the far end of the room rests two doors positioned at a forty-five degree angle above the floor. He looks over at a wall of skateboards then turns to a wall holding mountain boards. Running his fingers down the wall, he grabs a

17

translucent one with clear gripping wheels. He walks over to the angled doors, dropping the board to his feet. Falling forward into a pushup position, taking hold of a door handle in each hand, he takes a deep breath in, letting his chest drop to the surface of the doors. In one motion, he launches his body back upward, pulling the handles with him, swinging the doors open. A gust of sandy wind sends him flailing back as morning desert air fills the cabin lead by arid rays of sun.

Wheeler peers out below to a steep decline of desert hillside. He kicks up the lip of his board, snatching it out of the air. Taking one last look at the unmarked path below, he tosses the mountain board out into the world, leaping far out behind it. Landing with his feet shoulder length apart on the board an instant before it makes contact with the sloping desert hillside, knees bent low to the ground, leaning forward, he absorbs the shock of gravity. Speeding down the winding sandy rock slopes, he twists and slides along, avoiding cacti and desert trees standing guard. He sees a challenging change in terrain down ahead. He veers off the path, spraying sand and gravel. Weaving through camouflaged trunks and tall stems, he approaches a sendoff mound, howling out loud. Getting serious air, Wheeler looks down on patches of soft sand. He flips forward through the crisp air, tumbling upright on his board. He conforms to the leveling slopes slowing his momentum ahead, and slides to a bumpy stop.

Observing the landscape, Wheeler scopes a monumental wheel-shaped stone peeking out from the edge of a desert valley. He pushes on and in his peripheral vision locates something or someone, a grown coyote, gnawing on the neck of a bloody carcass behind a tree. The coyote looks up, quickly sniffing for clues as Wheeler whistles by on his board. He turns to face Wheeler with veiny yellow eyes and blood dripping from his flesh tearing teeth. The coyote starts after him, first trotting then running faster. Wheeler kicks to the ground as quickly as he can, but from the cloud of dust left from his four spinning wheels the coyote emerges fast on his trail. Wheeler slides to a halt, spraying sand and dirt in front of him. The coyote is looking dead ahead at him, less than ten meters away. Panting out loud, Wheeler desperately jumps off, stumbling back to grab his board by the trucks with both hands. Crouching low as the coyote leaps with his mouth wide open, Wheeler whips the board around, punching his arms to full extension. The hard lip meets the coyote's face, cracking his drooling jaw as teeth spew from his mouth. The coyote bounces limply off to the side in the direction of the blow as Wheeler falls to the ground with his heart pounding like a deer skin drum. Looking around with his pupils dilated, dry heaving in shock, he glances dreadfully at the deceased creature. Sitting down next to the coyote, breathing steadily to get his heart rate back to normal, Wheeler swirls his fingers slowly and curiously through the sand in front of him. Lying flat on his back, the sun's rays bend and crawl through the darkness behind his shut eyes.

Wheeler sits up, rubbing his face, recounting the violent encounter. He stands up scowling at the animal, inhaling deeply, gathering phlegm in his throat. He spits on the ground beside the corpse and walks away with his mountain board in hand. The coyote fades into the distance where his soul sets back out into the grand old yonder until wildlife come out from where they

19

hide to feast on one who preyed on them. Looking towards the edge of the valley, Wheeler drops his board and skates onward. Just up ahead sits the giant stone in the shape of a wheel shoved into the hillside. He stops, picking up his board to walk the rest of the way towards the stone with a disturbed and prideful demeanor glimmering across his white, straight-toothed smile.

Approaching the boulder disguised in the towering valley wall above him, Wheeler feels the sun burning hot on his neck as he turns to catch a glimpse of its white circular body shining brightly, blinding his view of the sky. Silky rays sparkle and pierce the chiseled spokes of the wheel-shaped stone as Wheeler stands at arm's length conforming his hands along the solid curves. He presses his palm to a hidden display screen and a graphing scan of his palm lights up green.

Leaning his back up against the valley wall, Wheeler pulls out the notebook from his backpack. He sits flipping through pages completely full, front and back, with diagrams of different trick ideas, skate parks, and equations noted around every image. He flips to the back where he pulls out a folded note taped to the last page which has an unfinished map outlining a triangular trade route between Hollywood, Santa Monica, and Venice. Wheeler flips back through the notebook reading outlines of intricate skate parks for multiple terrains and doodles of himself with Skate Masters first place trophies. He pulls out a pen and starts adding details to the latest doodle of himself next to the first place trophy for the rapidly approaching Skate Masters event. Soon pages in his notebook start to flutter. Looking up, covering the sun's shine with his arm, he watches through whirling sand as a helicopter descends beside him.

Wheeler stretches his arms to the sky, tucks his notebook away and runs over to the helicopter. Leaving the bloody mountain board behind with the desert, he swings the door open to find a female pilot with long dark hair waving beside her ear muffed headset and aviator sunglasses. He hops in the cockpit and leans in to kiss her for a long second. Slamming the door shut, their ascent begins. Turning around to the shallow rear of the helicopter, he rips red curtains apart to where two women wearing not much at all are sitting on a bed stretched to the edges of the remaining cargo space.

Rex wakes up laying in the sand gripping the neck of an empty sun-kissed champagne bottle. He lifts the bottle above his face, blocking late morning. Pouring out the last drops, liquid finds every part of his face except for his wide-open mouth. He jumps up, sniffling and rustling, rubbing his face and eyes. Looking around he notices the first bar he walked into the night before with an illuminated "cocktails" sign. He sees his skateboard resting wheels up on the shadowed side of a building. He hobbles over and attempts to skate on the beachside sidewalk. Wobbling frantically, he loses his balance as the skateboard flings out in front of him, crossing the street airborne and sending him twirling back through the air. He lands face first in the sand. His skateboard crashes through a glass window on the second floor of an apartment unit. Appearing at the window is a middle-aged man. He looks down through the shattered glass at Rex. He says nothing and just lights a cigarette. Rex stands up, shaking and spitting out sand. He flags down an approaching cab as he stumbles across the street to retrieve his skateboard returned by the man with a lit cigarette. Rex opens the passenger door hiccupping involuntarily, placing both hands on his knees. While vomiting on the curb, the cab slowly pulls away. Rex stands up on his skateboard. Holding his arms out for balance, stepping one foot down on the very back of the board's deck, front wheels lifting off the ground, he points the board due north. Dropping his other foot to the front of the deck, the wheels smack the sidewalk, nudging him forward.

Rex skates the short journey from Venice to Santa Monica back towards his penthouse, mind and body exhausted. He rubs his eyes in hopes of hangover relief when the aroma of burning cannabis fills the air around him. He drops his fists from his eyes noticing three young men dressed in designer brands sitting on a low wall that meanders along the beach sidewalk. They look up at him slowly rolling by. Rex smiles, giving them a thumbs up. Puffing and passing joints they wave him over. The one sitting in the middle is holding a black and red snakeskin backpack in his lap. Pushing one of his associates to scoot over he taps the seat next to him for Rex to join in. He unzips the top of his backpack enabling Rex to peek inside. A vacuum sealed plastic bag the size of a bed pillow filled with cut cannabis flower lay nestled inside. Pulling a switch blade out of a zippered pocket he slices open the bag releasing a mesmerizing aroma. Rex is handed a lit joint as he sits observing the vivid colors of herbal nugs inside the bag. He coughs harshly grinning and nodding his head in astonishment at the effects this particular strain of cannabis has on his body and mind. They grin at Rex's positive reaction and begin telling of their involvement in the cannabis industry. Growing weed in Northern California with dispensary locations throughout the state, they have established a popular brand identity tied to their coveted cannabis products. They also operate discretely by distributing their products nationally utilizing decoy shipping containers and hiding the profits by strapping cash to human mules traveling back and forth through airports. Rex is offered an endorsement opportunity promoting their brand as a pro skater. He has no answer for them. They encourage Rex to join them for brunch at a restaurant within walking distance. On the way, they brag about the strippers they brought back to their mansion and how one of the escorts stole the young man with the backpack's rare coupe last night during his party. As they make progress towards the restaurant some passersby yell to them acknowledging their superior role in the retail marijuana industry. Others recognize Rex as the famous skater while he swerves on his skateboard keeping pace with the three young men walking next to him.

Approaching from the opposite direction is the voice of someone babbling excitedly. Speaking, yet on the verge of screaming, a young man wearing dirty technicolored shorts and a ripped tie-dye t-shirt makes himself known to those within a social radius. People passing by are either laughing quietly to themselves or completely changing their path to avoid interaction with him. He's yelling enjoyably at every person he walks past. Hollering sporadically about end times and the power of disillusionment with the full expression of his natural aura turned up to a blinding capacity. As their paths are about to meet, the vibrant young man yells at one of the two associates exclaiming his resemblance to a famous wrestler. He mimics the wrestler's voice and staple attack move and they all burst out laughing. His widened eyes and red-faced hysterical smile give them all goosebumps as they approach the restaurant. The young man with the backpack turns around to face Rex, putting a finger to the tip of his tongue, raising an eyebrow as he does, hinting to Rex that the person they just encountered is tripping on LSD.

The four of them sit down at an outdoor table. Rex looks to the crashing waves between slits of bicyclists, skaters, and walkers passing by between the beach and shops as the young men dressed in their own brand's attire stare with blazed eyes at the menu. Rex sees an obese man who appears to be schizophrenic sitting on the concrete ground with his back resting against the beams of a gazebo and a skateboard rolling back and forth under his feet. The man looks down at the ground cocking his neck and jaw while widening and closing his eyes. His body moves fluidly to the rhythm of his restless voice.

They light a joint at the table swaying Rex's focus from the man by the gazebo. After everyone takes a puff, one associate walks over to the man under the gazebo with the joint in hand. They exchange some words before he hands over the joint and walks back to the table. Rex adjusts his seat observing the man under the gazebo inhale tedious puffs of smoke then peers down at the menu. The heavyset man elevates the octave of his voice into a more desperate calling after

24

the wind. Not moving from his seeping position on the floor, he remains stationary under the gazebo with gravity's tight grip conjoining him to the concrete. The man's head sinks to rest on his shoulder, gazing beyond puffs of dense smoke floating in and out of the coming ocean air. They laugh quietly at the change in the man's state of mind as he appears to be feeling better. Turning back to the table, a waitress comes by to take their order. Another young couple walking by points to the young men, recognizing them for their cannabis brand's success and waving with respect. The two associates take phone calls, wandering back and forth from the sidewalk to the table. The food portions are plentiful, so they fill up two to go containers of leftover food as the the young man with the backpack insists on paying the check. They walk over to the man under the gazebo, handing him one of the leftover food containers. He's thankful not shying away from vocalizing his appreciation for them brightening his day.

Strolling back in the direction of where they initially met, one of the associates strays from the group in a straight line toward someone hidden in a sleeping bag on the grass along the way. He places the second to go food container next to the person's head, walking fast again to rejoin the group. The associate pacing next to Rex turns suddenly into a beachside restaurant. The other two, walking ahead, look back at Rex, signaling for him to join them. The young man with the backpack tells Rex they have many collection points in small businesses running throughout Los Angeles. Rex is left walking next to him as the two associates weave in and out of beachside restaurants and shops.

Rex is invited to ride with him to check out the dispensary headquarters, which is also a storefront, clothing factory, and grow operation. The young man pulls a rare sports car key out of his backpack and tosses it to Rex. Stepping off his skateboard with a tired smile on his face, Rex throws the key back to him as they walk over to the red coupe. Rex opens the passenger door carefully trying not to scratch the bottom on the street curb. As he shuts the door the ignited engine awakens with a growl then settles into a powerful hum that can be heard from around the block. The young man recklessly accelerates out of his parallel spot with minimal space to maneuver, slamming them back into their seats then thrusting them forward having to brake behind heavy traffic blocking the ocean front avenue. Rex smiles over the loud engine shutting his eyes. The two associates climb into an inconspicuous car and follow after them.

Driving only a couple of miles in twenty minutes, the young man gets a call from his two associates requesting to stop at a nearby gas station. Rex remains seated in the coupe's passenger seat as the three of them speak outside. Rex stares absently being stoned, hungover, and aloof to the Skate Masters event set to ensue in only a couple of days. Attempting to curl up in the passenger's seat, he day dreams of dropping into mountain-high halfpipes, slicing through skate bowls covering wide valleys and gaining enough air to get stuck in orbit, holding the tail of his skateboard waiting to drop back down to Earth. Transcending that dream he remembers the most beautiful young woman he has ever seen peering down on him at the skate bowl in Venice. He's pulled back to reality when the young cannabis CEO re-enters the vehicle. Rex realizes he does not know the young man's name. None of them ever revealed their names. He looks at Rex apprehensively telling him they need to make another stop before heading to the dispensary headquarters. He pulls the red coupe out of the gas station, money-motivated music vibrating heavy bass out the windows, drifting onto the street.

They head to Beverly Hills from Santa Monica stopping at a coffee shop along the way. It's crowded inside, so the three young men ask Rex to order coffee for them before walking outside to sit at a table. Standing in a long line waiting to order, Rex contemplates his situation and relationship with them. He turns to look outside as they look uneasily inside at him. Rex turns hesitantly back to the coffee line with a confused look on his face. The exhausting sound of a monstrous pickup truck jacked up with spiked rims and human sized tires parks outside the coffee shop. A young man jumps down out of the driver's seat joining the three of them at the outside table. All four of them look uneasily at Rex through the glass. Rex stands there pretending not to notice. He finally gets the coffee that he has no interest in. Walking outside to join them, he sees there is nowhere for him to sit and the deliberate silence makes it clear they do not intend to make room for him. After initiating an awkward goodbye, Rex walks down the street, out of sight. He slowly comes to a stop realizing he left his skateboard in the red coupe. Shaking his head, unwilling to go back for it, he notices a parked cab on the other side of the street.

The cab driver pulls around to Rex's waving arm. Once Rex hops in the driver immediately tells Rex about how efficient his hybrid car is for the job. Rex chuckles and closes his eyes, just relieved to be on his way. The cabbie turns around with a brilliant smile on his face, staring at Rex. Sensing eyes on him, double-taking, Rex smiles curiously. The driver turns back around and starts to pull away. He reveals himself to be "Sungrab," a monk native to Tibet and relatively new to Los Angeles. He speaks to Rex about the life of a monk. Rex listens intently, sensing a positive energy radiating from the man. Sungrab tells him that all prayer is like cuisine. All sprawling lands and widespread cultures, every society and each community prepare for the feast of life and although resources are varied and unique the ritual serves the same purpose, to replenish both body and soul. Rex reflects in appreciation, meditating on the opportunity to meet Sungrab. When the cab arrives in front of Rex's flat Sungrab turns around to face him. Admiring Rex's desire to listen, Sungrab tells him that all of life occurs in one bright instant and he must trust himself to catch and release the light. Rex steps out of the car with a smile, and they bow with respect to one another through the open passenger side window.

        The most beautiful young woman Rex has ever seen sits amidst the steep and sprawling steps of Hollywood's City Hall. Eating a hotdog purchased from the sizzling snack stand below, she peers out at the hustle and bustle of pedestrians walking the streets. The tiring afternoon sun peeks out from within a maze of tall buildings shining ribbons of gold onto strips of the city. She squints her strained eyes while breathing in the polluted and arid air of central Hollywood, organizing a tall stack of flyers in the rustling breeze. She turns to the flashing commotion derived from the swinging open doors at the entrance to City Hall. Wheeler attempts to breakaway down the sprawling staircase where cameras and microphones swarm after him. He glances from side to side, moving fast to stay in front of the mob following him down the steps. He catches a glimpse of her eating a hot dog, surrendering at the sight of her with the widest of eyes. She stops eating for a moment, looking back at him. His eyes sparkle then sink, losing focus of his surroundings. His fast-moving feet transform to jelly, immersed in a world made solely of affectionate vibrations. Mind in a lovestruck daze, he trips over his own foot, falling graciously into the awaiting arms of his massive security guard. Startled back to reality, he searches for her face. The security guard opens the passenger door to a black SUV and props his limp body up in the backseat. Wheeler presses his face and palms up against the window looking for her again, cameras flash pictures of his face smudged up against the glass.

Wheeler turns away from the window with his heart in hand, startled to see the confused look on his family's faces. Two security guards sitting up front with Wheeler sitting in the middle row, his parents and siblings filling the remaining seats, all staring blankly at him. Wheeler looks back at them concerned, patting his security driver on the shoulder. The driver slams on the brakes, pulling over to the side of the city street. Wheeler and his security guard step out of the vehicle. Wheeler's father sticks his head out the window, pointing to his watch, patting the face a few times with his index finger, then pointing directly at Wheeler before the SUV pulls around the corner.

Wheeler walks in a hurry with the tails of his trench coat flailing in the breeze. He's wearing a t-shirt, shorts, tube socks, skate pads and brand new kicks. His three hundred pound security guard moves on his blindside, dressed in a pinstriped suit, sharp black shades and a communication earpiece, not to mention a tongue piercing. Wheeler stops dead in his tracks, looking around to find the best route back to City Hall. He runs for a couple of blocks, not stopping for traffic, zigzagging between cars and people until reaching the base of the grand staircase at City Hall. Scanning the faces of those above him, he discovers that she is no longer there. Looking down at his phone, he sees a text sent from his father. The message displays a photo of a watch with a finger pointed at it. He shakes his head in disapproval as his security guard catches up to him, panting from exhaustion with hands on his knees. Wheeler removes the trench coat, tossing it at his security guard, who snatches it out of the air and throws it over his shoulder. He extends a hand and his guard pulls out of his jacket pocket what appear to be two gun magazines. Wheeler plants one of the magazines on the bottom of his shoe, sliding the edge along the length of his foot until it clicks, then slides it back exposing five inline skate wheels secured to the bottom. He repeats the process for his other foot. He presses his fingerprint on his phone screen, unlocking a bar code that he scans along the length of his shoe, initiating a high-pitched sound of an electric battery charging up. He looks up at his security guard, lifting an eyebrow in heightened anticipation. He bursts forward, torso thrown back, speeding off down the road, brushing between pedestrians and cars. Whooshing around the block, people holler and shout as he whizzes through the densely populated streets, sparks shooting from his military-grade wheels with every cutting move and blazing step.

Wheeler stops at an intersection with buildings on each corner rising high into the clouds. He closes his eyes tightly, taking deep breaths as he shakes out his limbs. He feels his heart pounding at an accelerated rate. He opens his eyes, rolling towards police barricades blocking off the intersection. He slowly turns to enter the next street and is met by an eruption of applause as those lining the sidewalk notice him.

Blocked off intersections stretch far in front of Wheeler. He looks ahead to see a beautifully graffitied arrow painted down the full length of the pavement leading up to a massive metallic black vertical ramp standing ominously in position. He lights up at the cheering crowd as excitement bounces off flashing walls of the lining buildings. His eyes slit into focus watching the setting sun melt under the center of the ramp's peaked edge. Fireworks boom as he jolts forward.

At a dangerously high speed, Wheeler swings his arms and legs in fluid motion. Bending his knees with feet close together, he approaches the colossal ramp. An illuminating design comes to life at each passing section of the ramp's surface like a monstrous wave of art supercharging upward. He bullets up the steeping curve, spine nearly parallel to the street below. He takes flight, turning people into specks, seeing the tops of buildings out of his distorted peripherals and unbounded mind. Flipping and twirling over the fading echo of voices far below, in calculating descent, he lands on the counter side of the ramp. Left foot swerving without full control, he swishes down the slope. He waves his limbs to regain balance, shifting from one flailing foot to the other. He skids off center of the intended finishing area, dropping to his padded knees, sliding diagonally towards the finishing point. Digging into the pavement as fans standing behind the roped off area extend their hands, nicking his helmet and shoulders, he slides to a gradual halt. Body settling within inches of a pregnant woman holding a baby in each arm, his final momentum causes his face to gently make impact with her pregnant belly. The baby kicks against his sweaty cheek and the mother pronounces it to be the baby's first kick. The crowd erupts with shouts and applause as those witnessing leap and embrace one another. Hands from behind the ropes shake Wheeler's head and shoulders as those watching at home and on the giant city wall monitors see his luminous smile flashing for the cameras.

In the quietest spot of his beachfront flat, Rex sits cross-legged on a hardwood floor with his eyes shut and mind inwardly placed. Beams of light shine straight through the broad glass windows as he sits breathing steadily without making a sound. He absorbs the sun hitting him. His mind frees one memory after the next, suspended within the vast ocean of his mind, waves of past experiences wash over the rotating planes of his expanding focus. Rex takes in one exaggeratedly long breath after another until his lungs are fully expanded. Holding in his breath, he feels a steady pulse gently knocking within his head. He thinks about the Skate Masters event that is only two short days away. He imagines each motion of his routine going impeccably as the crowd cheers him on. He bends forward out of his crisscross position and begins to do push-ups. He loses himself in muscular strain and rhythmic breathing, his arms jittering to complete one final push-up. Reclaiming his meditative seated position, he focuses on the booming sensation in his head faintly making its way back into the recesses of his body. He peeks through watering eyes, making out the blurry shapes of speckling furniture in his penthouse before his eyes shut for good, unaware of a firetruck passing by as loud sirens whisper away with the wind.

Rex's mind drifts over the horizon of his consciousness, far away over deep waters, beyond the visual image, to someplace real. He breathes deeply within a dream, to a world within himself with no obvious ends. He sits in the sand, hair fluttering in the rampaging wind, struggling to see through grains of sand whizzing around his face. He puts up his arm to deflect the pelting specks. Rising up, he walks toward the white waves of the sea. Head down and eyes closed, drawn into shallow depths, raising his feet up out of the unsteady soaking sand, he falls forward, face spearing through cold salt water and body engulfed in the constant motion around him. The beat of coming waves pulse over his suspended body. Far away into the mind he bobs with the tides. Falling above and below, struggling against the shifting surface, his wet head roams in the windy air as the shore furthers from his sight.

The waves have grown in size as Rex drifts further out to sea. Diving down under with his kicking feet last to feel the chilly air, he sees a school of fish swimming just beneath him. Bright scaly bodies shimmer in the foggy salt water, scurrying away from his diving arms, revealing a deep gap between his suspended body and the sandy ocean floor. Rex swims down to the settling sand. Burying his hands and arms, he maneuvers his lower body down to the sea floor, holding his core still against the movement of waves. He closes his eyes tighter, searching to find somewhere else to go, when an anchor plummets into the sand beside his settled body.

Bellowing his arms up out of the sand and crouching low to the sea floor, Rex shoots straight up out of the ocean, hovering high above a rotting old fishing boat rocking to the storming song of the sea. In his descent, he looks to the captain's chair of the boat, locking eyes with a man wearing a bright yellow fishing coat and long grey beard. Rex plummets down into the ocean, staring back up at the fishing boat hanging above him, moored on a line of rusted chain, yanking back and forth, soon to unhinge the overworked anchor. He swims to the surface, paddling his way half-blind in the splashing rain to a ladder on the stern of the boat. Soaked from head to toes, he climbs each step. He sees the boat captain's yellow coat standing over him. A hand reaches down like a claw. Rex grabs the hand with a suctioning grip before he's swung over the edge onto the boat deck. He's astonished to find his feet landed safe and sound. Peering up, shaking blankly in the pouring rain, he stares at the boat captain who has the skin of fire burnt salmon and the eyes of a mad sailfish. The captain scurries his way past Rex to raise the anchor. The boat shifts from side to side as Rex struggles to find his footing without falling overboard. The waves have grown in size behind the captain, whose face is buried under a flask of rum spilling out over his rosy cheeks onto the soaked deck, singing in sailor slang to the sound of the pounding storm. At the climax of his song, he drops to his knees, belting out the words that seem to form an overwhelming wave rooting beneath the boat. They begin to rise up as the wave rains down on the deck. The boat rotates, pulling higher into the tidal wave. Rex runs to man the wheel. The heavy wooden steering wheel rocks and spins. The captain jolts from his liquor, his hip knocking Rex over the side of the boat into the rushing sea storm. From the top of the wave, its inevitable tumble begins. Rex crashes down within the wave's break, barreling in the dark blue undercurrent, his senses powerless, numbing him into the depths of pure experience. He's finally spit out of the rumbling wave left sleepy and weak. Floating to the surface of a calm grey day, he shuts his restless eyes, the sound of the captain's song whistling away over the horizon.

A faint knock at the door is followed by a small head hesitantly making way into Rex's flat. Unaware of the visitor's entrance, Rex drops to his chest to do push-ups. The boy stands inside the flat watching him. Rex peers up from the ground at him. Smiling delicately, he jumps upright turning to open doors leading out to a balcony facing the beach. The boy follows Rex outside, looking wide-eyed at the glimmering ocean flowing in a magical cadence. He observes Rex about to light a cigarette. Flickering it on his lips in contemplation, Rex drops his hands and spits the cigarette out over the ledge to the dusty sidewalk. He steps over to the lounge chairs facing out and the boy climbs into a chair next to him. They sit there watching the sunset and within moments Rex looks over to see the boy has fallen asleep. He pulls the mattress out from the couch to make a bed for the boy. Rex picks him up and the boy hugs him around the neck without waking an eye. Rex tucks him under the covers and steps back. He bumps into a liquor bottle, his lightning-fast reflexes react as he snatches the glass bottle out of the air before it shatters on the hardwood floor. He looks at the half-empty bottle wondering why he made such an effort to save it. Going to take a swig, he sees the boy asleep out of the corner of his eye. Dropping his arm, he decides to go off to bed instead.

When Rex awakens, he finds the boy is nowhere to be found. All of the drawers are pulled out, each cushion turned over, cupboards swung open, yet all valuables remain. He rolls his eyes in despair, applying pressure to his forehead with the palms of his hands. He tries to think hard about something to do but can't help laughing. He starts his day bemused, performing his morning routine, stepping around the subtle tornado caused by the boy. Brushing his teeth and working through a light stretch with breakfast in hand, he makes his way out to see what the day has in store for him. He swings the door open to discover a cute young woman with a distressed smile standing in his way. Surprised, Rex coughs and a bite of breakfast shoots out of his mouth into the hall. Her timidity turns to ferocity, nimbly lunging at him. Wrapping her arms and legs around his waist, she kisses all over his body. Rex throws the rest of his food into the hall. Banging against the walls with pictures falling down, he reciprocates her passion. They make their desperate way, ripping off each other's clothing as he carries her to the master bedroom. Rex swings the door shut behind him. They moan and groan during the daylong lovefest until they are both completely spent. Laying in the hot bed, Rex gets a call. He takes his phone and throws it out the broad window toward the busy beach, cutting into the soft sand, landing dangerously close to a man laying out with large headphones, pleasantly unaware of the glass brick thrown carelessly near his fragile bald head.

Finding their way back under the covers, minds and hearts meshing in a kaleidoscope of flesh as late afternoon transitions softly to evening, concluding lights of the day crash through the window, smashing into their bare shoulders while rolling waves bang and drip from cliff walls. Rex goes to grab a cigarette and notices the pack is empty. He goes to make a drink and realizes all of the alcohol has been poured out. Stepping back to the bedroom he finds her gone.

Feeling out of touch, Rex bolts down to ground level. He strolls the street with hazy vision, the world flowing by in globs of color. He suddenly freezes up, instinctively hopping out of the way of a skateboarder zooming by on the sidewalk beside him, spinning back the other way to avoid being trampled by a couple running by pushing baby strollers. Rex looks frantically in each direction for the next looming obstacle, but nobody else is nearby. He lets out a sigh, stretching down to his toes, closing his eyes, letting his arms dangle. Rising back up with bloodshot eyes, he starts back toward the side alley of his residential building. He walks the sun-kissed road down into the garage where his sleek matte lime green two-seater is parked in the back corner. He starts up the engine, music blasting, quickly pushing the volume nob to mute. Taking a deep and determined breath in, silently exhaling his winded thoughts, he pulls out of the airy residential alley onto the beachfront street. There are not many cars on the road with few people scattered about the shops and paths leading to the beach. Rex pulls up to a red light focusing his energy in the present moment. A loud purring engine pulls up beside him. Inside the red sports coupe is the young man with the snakeskin backpack. He has a young woman curled up on his lap in the driver's seat and one of his associates sitting shotgun with a young woman on his lap. Rex makes eye contact with him. He signals with a sharp look for Rex to follow them. The streetlight turns green and the red coupe tears through the road ahead. Rex drops his head, exhaling for a long second before chasing after them.

Winding their way up and down through town, they finally stop in front of the cannabis brand's headquarters. Dozens of people are waiting along the entrance to the building. They give their keys to the valet and walk straight in. Inside the building are three open elevations of all white, state of the art architecture. The first floor is the most industrious area of the facility with a large room beyond the foyer where customers can look through shelves on the walls to a garden of hemp plants and automated growing equipment located behind the long counters which are full of branded THC and CBD products. Rex inhales the earthy air cycling throughout the facility, walking along with uncertain expectations. He follows the young man with the backpack up a wide spiraling staircase. Winding their way up, Rex looks to the second floor. He observes the stitching and printing machines laid out across tables full of sketches and prototype clothing designs, accompanied by original art surrounding them in a creative loft of productivity. Rex steps up to the third floor, examining a clear dome ceiling with an abstract woven canopy stretching over them. It's a grand office for the young cannabis CEO with panoramic views of Beverly Hills.

A security guard comes up to Rex, frisking his body for wires and weapons. He grabs Rex's wallet which Rex snags right back, turning away and throwing the wallet back over his head at the guard, he plops down on the elegant suede sofa which curls like a plush slug in the center of the office. The young man comes to sit down next to Rex, signaling for the guard to bring him his backpack. The guard scans Rex's ID, flicking the wallet back at him, before retrieving the backpack.

Unzipping his backpack, the young man removes an herb grinder from within a side pocket. Twisting it to-and-fro, opening up the top compartment, he taps bits of weed into a king-sized rolling paper. Acquiring a small filter, rolling it into the shape of a "W," he neatly wraps the end closest to him, curling it upward as the crease hugs to the circular filter. He licks the glue on the edge of the paper, rolling from the bottom tightly over the filter, then twisting the wrapped cannabis into a perfectly tapered cone. He sparks the top edge of the joint, fire dwindling down, cannabis ablaze. He inhales slowly, letting a tiny cloud of smoke escape from his mouth before vacuum sucking it back in. He holds the smoke in his lungs for longer than he can take. His face turns bright red, coughing violently, smoke disperses in rapid gusts from his drooling mouth. He coughs hard, holding the joint in one hand with his other hand making a fist in front of his mouth like a microphone. He hands the joint to Rex with a melted smile pinned across his face. Rex takes the joint from him, breathing in a smooth prolonged drag of smoke. He holds the hit in, closing his eyes, letting it creep out of his mouth at a steady pace, coughing once at the tail end of the smoke's departure from his lips. He sits back and closes his eyes to the company, basking in the flow of the moment.

Rex opens his eyes to the young CEO pacing across the office on his phone with one of his associates following intrusively behind attempting to listen. As the young man stomps about, Rex looks around curiously, noticing a tighter spiraling staircase in the corner of the office. He walks over, looking down the swirl of stairs, startled by a door opening at the very bottom, where a security guard barges out from a hidden room. In a startling glimpse, Rex sees naked women with masks and gloves sorting large mounds of powder through the closing door. A guard comes up behind Rex and grabs him by the arm. Rex swings around, slashing at the guard's grasp upon him. Breaking free, he turns the other way, flicking the guard off. Gliding quickly down the wide-open spiraling staircase, briskly moving through the dispensary, Rex exits the building and presents the valet ticket out front. He goes unnoticed by the young man with the backpack hurrying out the front door with his two associates following closely behind before hopping into an inconspicuous car and speeding off.

She springs one foot at a time, bounding her way beneath the gleaming stars and bright lights radiating from the Pacific Wheel at Santa Monica Pier. Watching passive waves lean upon the sand, she looks out at fog covering the ocean. Searching deep into the dense air, with no horizon in sight, she breezes her way along, gazing at gift stands closing down for the night. Music playing there earlier in the day, a crate for a stage, every twenty feet or so, upon which artists play for the people that come to explore the attractions. Floods of transient sounds interact over the edges of the wood plank straightaway. Each musician captures a brief audience within a jam space, offering original tunes to those strolling along the boardwalk. An older woman in a worn coat remains at the end of the pier with her possessions bundled on a broken cart. At the furthest point of the pier, sitting on two crates, she whistles her flute in harmony with the crashing waves as the young woman stands somewhere behind her watching imaginatively.

She looks down, sniffling at the stack of flyers in her hands, twirling her fingertips around the outline of a boy's face in the printed photo. Spinning lights of the empty Ferris wheel reflect clearly off teardrops drowning her enchanted eyes. She looks beyond the pier, deep into the foaming fog. She heads toward the pier's entrance where a conjoining circular path leads in all directions back into the world. Turning south, she's held up by a gust of whirling wind. Gazing up at the stars, shivering in her loose jacket, she carries on posting a flyer to every street post.

Following the winding sidewalk, she moves out of the way of bicyclists, scooters, and skaters, only a block away from a motel where she's been lodging. She looks up suddenly, turning to where three young men dressed in designer brands are sitting on a low wall along the beach. Two of them, attention lost to their phones, do not see her, but the young man sitting in the middle holding a backpack in his lap is staring right at her. She sees his hand rise up and mouth begin to move as she turns away from him in the direction of the motel. He appears abruptly in front of her, his smile arrogant and unnaturally straight. She swallows frightened, searching for a way out. His physical expressions mirror her movements. Overcome by vertigo, her eyes spinning to the Ferris wheel lights, she punches him straight in the nose with one flashing blow. She brushes by his shoulder as he shouts out in pain, lifting his head up, bleeding all over his hands, clothing and backpack. She hurries through the frail motel doors, shaking her bruised hand, taking the slow rickety elevator. Entering her room, heart pounding, she walks slowly to the window, peering to the spot on the low wall where the young men had been sitting, but they're no longer around.

In his backyard abutting the beach, Wheeler sits facing the ocean. He observes the mounds of sand settling forever beyond his sight and comprehension. Looking deep into the fog-covered ocean, he ponders familiar figures amongst the dark clouds. His focus is broken up by two four-wheel bikes riding over the sand in his direction. Two officers pull up next to him. One of them hands him a flyer. An officer shines a flashlight onto the paper showing a picture of a lost boy, then shines the light in Wheeler's eye. Wheeler puts his arm up to block the beam. They jet off into the night, spraying sand in their wake. Wheeler stands up, spitting out sand. He runs across the backyard, approaching a large trampoline beside an Olympic-sized swimming pool. He back handsprings twice on the grass, propelling into a high backflip and sticking his landing at the trampoline's center. Ricocheting upwards, elevating to the top windows of his three-story home, he closes his eyes and releases the flyer from his grasp as it flutters out of the picture. He dives effortlessly, softly breaking the surface of the heated pool with perfect form, curling back upwards from within the calm depths. His head emerges for air, missing two young women in bikinis who crash through the water beside him, revealing their smiling identities beneath the scattering bubbles. Rising ecstatically, they giggle and splash with each other. A young woman standing by the bar inside the house shouts to the three of them to come take shots of tequila. One of the young women places her hands on the edge of the pool, pushing herself out. She walks over to a lounge chair and dries herself with a towel. Picking up her phone, she walks around to the front of the house.

Wheeler looks at the smiling young woman remaining with him in the pool. They splash playfully before swimming together to kiss. The young woman inside the house comes fast and shakily through the French doors to the patio holding a platter with five shots poured and cut lime wedges hanging on the glass rims. She takes one step too quickly in her high heels and the whole platter comes crashing down behind her. Almost falling in the pool, she catches herself at the last second, remaining upright and happy. Wheeler and the young woman hugging to his body are amused at the sight, sinking beneath the night air.

Voices echo through the home as Wheeler's family appears, standing bunched together, staring outside at them through a grand arching back window. They roll their eyes, silently dispersing to separate rooms of the estate, except for Wheeler's father, who points to his watch and then at Wheeler, before disappearing into the mansion. The young woman, still drying her hair, reappears from the side of the house with a young man walking beside her, their arms interlocked. Wheeler and the young man wave to each other as the two young women by the pool hoot words of welcome to him. All three young women make their way just inside the house to make drinks at the expansive granite bar. Wheeler stands in the shallow end of the pool, about to get out and join him on the deck, when the young man taps his shirt pocket, lifting a finger for Wheeler to wait, then lightly jogs back around the side of the house. Wheeler walks over the backyard, looking out to rumbling black lids and white lashes of rolling waves. Closing his eyes, he listens to the benign crashing of the ocean beneath him, breathing in salty air, squeezing and releasing his toes in the sand. His senses shift, indulging in the aroma of perfume glinting through the night breeze. Turning away from dark skies over the ocean, he walks toward the young women inside by the bar as the young man reappears from the side of the house with a plastic bag hanging out of his shirt pocket. Inside the house one of the young women hands Wheeler a glass of vodka on the rocks.

Wrapping her arm around his neck, she brands him with a lipstick kiss on the cheek, "Cheers!" They dance with their attentions preoccupied, taking long, smiling sips from their drinks before wobbling back outside. On the patio, the young man pulls out the bag from his shirt pocket revealing clear pills with pink crystallized powder filling up the bottom of each capsule. He gives a pill to each of the young women, their hands all cupped and ready, and one to Wheeler, who's somewhat reluctant to receive it. Lining up along the bar, placing their glasses down, they carefully open each capsule, letting pink sand pour into their crackling mixed drinks. Stirring the concoction with colorful twisty straws, they waltz their way out the front doors. One by one, Wheeler leads them down the steps to a horseshoe driveway where a limousine is waiting for them. Toppling over each other, attempting to find at least part of a seat, they sip their drinks and yell for music to be played. The driver slaps the radio on button and hypnotic trance music blasts out the windows. They dance to the music for one original mix track before arriving at an oval concert hall. Reposing in the foreground of the grand structure, a garden with precisely trimmed foliage spruces up along mazing paths leading to an auditorium.

They flood out of the limousine onto the sidewalk. The young man who provided the pink pills holds his arms above his head, waving yellow tickets in the air. The three young women grab at him, clawing harmlessly for a ticket. Struggling to give them each a pass, the young man trips over from the weight of the scrapping huddle, bringing them gradually to the ground. Buzzing from laughter, they resume an upright seated position on the sidewalk. Wheeler stands, extending his hands to help two of the young women up as the other one is lifted into the arms of the young man giving out tickets.

The two young women playfully fight and punch with Wheeler, grabbing him to follow them into one of the many entryways of the green architectural maze. Skipping along the graveled path, they kiss and slip, hugging and falling their way along. They playfully bring him down in the secluded chaos, unbuttoning his jeans. Wheeler holds onto gravel and sculpted tree roots for one of the best two minutes of his life. The young women look at each other, helping one another regain their composure as he sits hunched up against a bush with his pants around his ankles. One of the young women takes a closer interest in finding the correct way to the grand hall's entrance while the other one brands Wheeler with another lipstick kiss, clutching her purse in one hand and grabbing the back of his neck with her other arm. She straddles him on the fluid ground, pressing his face into her cleavage as he nuzzles deep within her breasts. She pulls out a thin strip of tie dye from her purse pocket, ripping off a sliver of cardboard and releasing his suctioning lips from her chest. Placing the colorful square under his tongue, removing her fingers from inside his mouth, she presses her index finger gently against his lips and kisses him.

Beneath the magnificent romantic mural of angels, embroidered in meticulous gold design, praising the heavens above, which covers the entirety of the oval dome enclosing the concert hall lobby, Wheeler sways loosely from his heels to his toes. With low fuzzy eyes and a bashful smile, he peers around, odd-balling the fancily dressed ticket holders coming in and out of the ornate, espresso-colored doors burnt with deep engravings upon rich sappy circles.

Wheeler blinks incoherently, intrigued by the trail of lights and sounds buzzing around him, existing in a conscious state much bolder and unruly than his sober persona. He holds his warm hand against one of the many white pillars stretching up like snowy willow trunks. Wheeler's other arm is wrapped around one of the young women. She's dancing quietly to herself, eyes shut in a rapid dream. Smiling, singing softly, she awakens at the chorus of her song, raising the octave of her voice, gripping Wheeler by the cheeks. She belts out the words, brushing his hair with her glittery palms, leaving specs of light on the tip of his nose and tiny flashing diamonds on top of his hair. The young man with the tickets appears with the other two young women, retreating from the concession bar holding as many drinks as they can carry. Arms linked, the five of them storm through one of the daunting doorways. Passing by hundreds of people, row after row, surrounded by balconies hanging off the baroque interior of the auditorium, they arrive at their seats. Five seats together, second row and center. Wheeler looks around at the sophisticatedly dressed patrons, hardly aware of any of them, especially the person sitting directly in front of him, a young man holding a snakeskin backpack in his lap.

The young man sitting next to Wheeler cups his hands over Wheeler's ear to whisper something. The lights dim and curtains draw. "You good?" the young man asks, smiling at Wheeler who chuckles dismissively, shying obliviously away from the young man's intensifying concern, hiding his fuzzy head in folded arms. Horns raised and string bows readied, the crowd's volume diminishes in suspense as spotlights dance upon the stage. The young women sitting next to Wheeler speak vivaciously to each other, falling over arm rests with knees on their seats, rubbing Wheeler's back to regain his attention. Wheeler sits still, eyes closed, visualizing deep within his subconscious. His imagination fixates on a focal dot of light suspended in a void of darkness. The glowing point begins to move. His perspective follows the white dot accelerating exponentially until it's traveling at incalculable speeds. Streaking strands of light appear. Bolts tear through the roots which bond space before the eye as the white point surpasses the speed of light. Wheeler follows, breaking out of space itself, shuttering remnants of a shooting star leave the image of an ember, a flower sown in magma and fire, resting in the inner-scoped fragments of his reality, reaching for the full elasticity of his mind's capacity. His perspective snaps back to his physical place in the world as he feels his shut eyes resting in his own arms and the tenderness of the young women beside him rubbing his back. Peaking from the psychoactive stimulant, which he gulped down like fish food in a glass bowl, Wheeler lifts his head looking around the dark and loud concert hall. He stands up abruptly. Waving off the confused objections of those he came with, he walks then jogs up the middle of the concert isle. Grazing the shadows of heads on either side of him, he continues frantically up the sloping red carpet with shifting pupils. Stopped by security before exiting past the broad espresso doors, detoured another way, he changes course without a word, back to his seat. They're relieved to see him return, welcoming him with hands of comfort. Wheeler nods with sweat on his smiling face, soon overcome by a stream of passing ideas about his current reality. One illustration after the next, appearing in a wheel of spirited animation, hurl him inwardly to feverish hallucination. The three young women whisper loudly to one another, trying to find a way to help him, when the young man with a designer brand backpack swirls around to face them. He rests his elbows over his seat, whispering something to one of the young women. Zipping open his backpack, he pulls out a pen, handing it to her and pointing to Wheeler, then turning back to face the grand performance ensuing on stage. The young woman lifts Wheeler's lazy-eyed head, placing the pen up to his mouth and whispering in his ear, "It's weed." Wheeler perks his head up, raising the pen carelessly, nicking his front tooth, mouth staggering to pucker over the mouthpiece of the cannabis oil filled pen. He puffs, blowing vapor smoke down by his feet, clouds disperse in musical notes beneath the orchestra performing on stage above them.

Music reaches to the ends of the curving architecture, swirling back around to lift Wheeler's head from his arms, as illusions, melting like a hot summer's day ice cream, fill his brain. Gleaming and swaying to the sad strings singing above him, he imagines a unique skate routine to win the world over at the imminent Skate Masters event. Rolling with the tides, swerving with the curving earth, he connects to his skateboard, etching the details of ramps and rails like a sculptor shaving away at marble medium, until the slashing brushes of black ink come closing in on him, constricting him in the fine curves of his own signature, the one that's bound him to the Skate Masters endorsers. His body slips through ink's grasp, breathlessly submerged in a deep well. Wheeler's eyes sparkle and shutter, beads of sweat line the edges of his face. He swipes his forehead, moisture dripping onto the floor in front of him, slipping into semi-consciousness.

Nearing the crescendo of the show, Wheeler nuzzles to the young woman in the seat to his right, head resting in her lap. She puts a straw up to his mouth and he distortedly sucks ice water down his throat. He suddenly grabs the glass out of her hand, the frigid contents pour on his face, seeping into her lap. With a cry, she stands up. Security moves in the direction of their row. Flashlights swarm and lights in the concert hall flicker on, announcing intermission. Ticket holders file out to the lobby. Security guards holding Wheeler by the arms lead the way as those he came with follow closely, and the young man with the backpack trailing behind them.

Ruffling the sloping red carpet, trudging through the forest of espresso-colored doors, Wheeler is tugged out by security. His swimming limbs struggle to avoid the audience blocking the aisle. A rotating spotlight from the highest balcony shines around the crowd, honing in on him amongst the huddle of glimmering dresses and exotic fabrics funneling between the imposing doorways, coalescing into feathery, flowing molasses. Wheeler looks up past the lights and escorting hands of security to the arbor carvings of the arched doors, mesmerized by the smooth oily vines blending cherry with charcoal. A man in peacock blows a mouthful of cigar smoke into the back of Wheeler's neck as they exit, inducing the impression that someone set the roots and vines of the doorway on fire. Wheeler looks back over his shoulder through the smoke, glancing above the buzzing heads.

The doors warp, releasing ashy spirits from the depths of wrinkling old tree trunks, taunting him in a maze of voices that shove him to the breeze, blowing him onto the broad steps, as he stumbles backwards. A black SUV pulls up and the rear passenger door swings open. Wheeler trips on the curb, fading into time levitating, his eyes in a fleeing trance. Outstretched hands sprout out from blossoming stems, wrapping around his limbs like preying snakes. They snatch his falling body out of the black air in one swift motion and the door shuts tightly behind his dreaming head.

Regaining consciousness inside the SUV, Wheeler tries processing his family staring blankly at him. He licks the sweat off his upper lip, closing his eyes again at the speed of a fluttering sheet falling to bed. He rocks himself back to the corner, between the seat and door, hitting his head with a dull thud as the driver jolts forward. Glimmers of telephone poles whooshing by and blurry lines of white light passing beneath his nose, Wheeler breathes against the window. Pupils dominate the whites of his eyes and his eyelids slither from side to side like plucking brass strings. He becomes activated when they stop at a gas station.

In one flailing swoop, Wheeler pounces out of the passenger side door, stumbling to run off down the residential street not far from his family's beachfront estate in Santa Monica. Running west towards the beach, he cuts south along the sandy sidewalk. Nearly deserted all around him, he catches his breath on a dead and buried LA night. Tripping upon a wooden bench, he lays down on the divided seat, staring to the interior of his eyelids before anxiously sitting up. His focus narrows on the idea of breathing. The clearly pronounced tones of snoozing waves, cold pink sweat drying along the corners of his forehead, the purple breeze of coming morning, consciousness lost.

    Rex steps out of a helicopter in the desert. He walks toward an airplane hangar camouflaged in ripples of endless sand. A massive half pipe rests in the middle of the open hanger. An iron chain hovers above the half pipe. Flickering murals glow on the surrounding walls from the light casted by hundreds of candles dripping hot wax into holsters of a two-century old chandelier. The Skate Masters emblem drapes down, masking corridors and tunnels interlocking the chambers of the hangar's underground. Rex walks to the center of the half pipe where the Skate Masters emblem is stamped in shimmering gold at the center of the ramp's base. Kneeling down, he presses his palm flat. A scanner recognizes his fingerprints and the ramp retracts from the center. A clear platform appears from beneath the ramp, revealing black and gold carpeting in the room one floor below. Rex steps on the platform and it lowers slowly to the ground. He observes a tunneled-out room with a low ceiling. A rectangular table and eight chairs are on the far side of the room. Seven of the chairs are occupied by significant members of the current Skate Masters endorsers and their legal counsels. Arguing on the edges of their seats, their voices fade to a bickering silence as he walks the length of the room.
    Rex observes the paintings along the walls which retain the story of a man who becomes lost to an

ambiguous storm. The paintings are meticulously preserved and each one is protected by an extravagant frame. The drowning man stares out from overwhelming depths through each portrait with confused and devastated eyes. Rex studies the paintings as he walks. Each one depicts the man above, below and between, an undefinable surface line and fluid background. Rex loses focus on the man in the paintings when he notices the black pearl of a smooth camera lens at the top center of each lavish and deteriorating portrait frame. He glances back to the table of men quietly waiting for him.

Rex walks up next to the empty chair, then leans over the iron table with both of his palms resting on the cold tabletop. Two of the Skate Masters endorsers slide a computer tablet across the table into his resting hands. Rex analyzes a contract printed on the screen. Gazing up at their elongated expressions, he moves his face and hands close to the tablet. Grabbing its corners, he spins it in place on the smooth table. He departs from them without signing at the very bottom of the contract. A murmuring upheaval of endorsers riot in objection as the computer tablet spins in place like a top. Rex only notices the last painting on the wall where the man from each of the previous paintings has vanished.

Rex steps again onto the elevator platform, looking back at the endorsers on the other side of the room, all of them rising from their chairs, leaning over to shake hands with one another from across the table, and coming to a sorted arrangement without him. Emerging up through the base of the halfpipe, Rex is triggered by skateboard wheels banging against the half pipe above him and sees a Skate Masters legend sitting over the edge of the ramp holding a skateboard vertically between his legs as he clanks the wheels against the ramp. Bursting up the side of the ramp, Rex puts his hand out for the legend to pull him up. They sit at the top of the ramp in the still airplane hangar looking out to the desert. Rex peers down through the center of the ramp where he just rejected a new endorsement deal with Skate Masters. He smiles at the legend and slides down the half pipe, his momentum guiding him out. "This whole organization is going to Hell," says the Skate Masters legend. Rex leaves the words behind in the early morning dew, brushing out of the hangar, beneath the night's leftover stars, kicking his feet through cosmic dunes to a helicopter awaiting his return.

Across the street from Wheeler's unconscious body, a red sports coupe pulls up in front of a closed restaurant along the Santa Monica coastline. Wheeler's day breaks open at the piercing force of one of the young men in designer brands revving up the powerful engine. Wheeler pukes, his face illuminated and fragile like a nauseous lava lamp. He falls to his hands and knees from the park bench, shattering the moment with his face dangling right above the sidewalk. He feels those sickening thoughts dissolve to zero as his perspective shifts to a lucid dream. Life hits him like lightning in a bottle. The scrolls of time unleash into his reality. He rises to his feet like it was only imagined. Head up and legs grounded in pursuit, destined in each step, he walks towards the beach, diagonally across from where unmarked duffle bags are being unloaded from the rare sports coupe.

Wheeler steps through the cool sand, each step revealing a vivid plane of experience, a new dream for every moment. He becomes lost within life, chasing his own becoming, eyes opened to a newfound key to knowledge. He steps into the street beside the beach, zooming in on two women riding bicycles smiling at him as they whiz past. Wheeler walks down the road with a rampaging smile, an uncovered sense of being. He speaks out in tongues, ranging from pirate improvisation to an unconvincing Jamaican accent. Running ahead, he jumps past a car coming down the road. He dodges right and then left. A sense of power from every element coercing through him. Stepping into a golden light formerly untouched, he takes off his shoes, throwing them to the ocean, leaving his pants hovering in a silk web of foaming waves. He stares facing out, watching the sun come up, rolling over in hours of sand. Gazing upon the illuminated waves, he watches intergalactic spaceships cruise just above the water with scorching white waves firing in their wakes. Rocketing sailboats and flying saucer sport yachts, infused with soft colors sent from the spectrum of all the sky's days, blasting before his eyes. As the last of the parade sails by, Wheeler looks down at his hands. He sees the colors of his skin in a transparent and unfamiliar light. Incited in his unsettlement, triggered by existential contemplation, "Why the world, between this time, living my life?"

A helicopter appears above the tall palm trees planted along the sandy paths, palms bristling and sand scribbling as one of Wheeler's security guards appears from inside the open helicopter, emerging from the depths of Hell, and in frantic desperation calls out to Wheeler through a megaphone. The helicopter jolts from a stirred obese man hurling bottles and cans from the steps of a gazebo. One of the bottles finds its mark on the security guard's head, who then drops the megaphone, bursting it to pieces. Wheeler flails from his crisscross position in the sand, running in all directions, naked in every sense of the word. The helicopter retreats as Wheeler runs down the bike path along the beach in the direction of his beachfront estate. His voice blurts out in tongues at the few scattered humans wandering in the quiet light of early morning.

The sun rises lazily by Wheeler's feet as he hops his way down an alley. He is startled by a rustling noise coming his way. A monstrous shadow appears on the wall of one of the lining buildings. Huddling beside a dumpster, heart pounding, he whispers in tongues. He draws on the dirty concrete ground, friction blistering his fingertips, awaiting his fate. A sullen man in ragged clothes suddenly appears from the opposite direction of the growing shadow. Wheeler lets out a frantic holler. The drunken man jumps up from the noise. Drool washes onto his limp hand as he staggers his way up the middle of the alley, a paint bucket he has been settling on for some time swings sullenly in his grasp through a torn glove. The drunken man limps past the dumpster without noticing Wheeler's squatted position. He slurs a bent warning in the direction of the shadow, throwing an empty bottle of scotch from within his bucket, shattering the glass as the shadow evolves on the alley wall. The drunken man hits the floor, crawling forward into a dark corner of the alley.

Wheeler looks in every direction, abandoning his hidden position and running back toward his family's estate.

The shadow changes form on the wall, revealing the silhouette of a boy. With the fingers of one hand extended through holes in his shorts pockets and the other hand holding his skateboard, he walks along with his feet kicking rocks in the dust. Looking up at balconies hanging over the alley, passing by windows to see people he will probably never know, safe and snug, only hoping one of the windows he gazes upon will resemble home. The boy drops his skateboard to the floor. Rolling over rubble until a flyer prevents his forward progress like a canoe hitting a soft ocean sandbar. He hops off the board to read the ripped and weathered flyer caught in his wheel. All that is left to read are the words, "Missing Child," above the edges of a cutoff photo. Adrenaline fills his eyes with night's pond. Scattering the dust, he gallops between the alley walls as his wheels roll over cracks in the sidewalk, mirroring his elevated heart rate. He escapes the tall alley walls. Reaching free air, inhaling the sun, he squints to the rising light of a coming day.

Wheeler walks along the sandy sidewalk beside the beach with his head up, thorns and pebbled rocks pricked in his bare feet, and his mind taking on dimensional understanding. Each thought and feeling liberated from the constraints of the ego, an inexorable flight into flowing, just as a spinning umbrella mists away fallen raindrops. Silently basking in the recesses of his being, the vision of his soul recollects the lost way of his true self, rejuvenating his reality in every soaking moment. The sun finds its way from the bottom of the horizon to just beneath the passing marshmallow clouds. Lines of sweat evaporating from his feverish head, he stops under the cool canopy of a deep-rooted tree in front of someone's estate. Placing his hand to his heart, he catches up with his tiredness. Tanning his shut eyelids, he chases beams of coming and going ideas, each one containing a path to follow, a new decision to chase down. Closing his eyes tighter, diving deeper into the infinite access of his perception, thoroughly engaged in connected experience, he rests under the tree, exploring his imagination as a phenomenon defined all throughout space and time. He opens his eyes, drawn back to unaltered reality, his great connection to all, seeping into the emergence of his habitual senses as the scrolls of time roll shut, leaving him with the solid fact that Skate Masters begins in less than a few hours.

Wheeler puts his palms upon exposed roots leading up the tree, inhaling rays of sun with accents of bark and salt, stepping along the inner roots, a model molded by gravity, on the way to his estate, no more than a quarter mile away. He walks as human, lion and sheep, when the infliction of a hornet stinger, assembled with cold metal tubing and feathered backing, penetrates his throttled neck. Falling to the sidewalk, he twists in one swift motion, rotating his body in free fall. His head misses the unforgiving pavement, landing upon a warm bed of front lawn as his eyes close in on the glimmering mess of starry leaves and shooting branches above.

Rex is dropped at a helipad on the roof of his penthouse in Santa Monica. He stuffs his pads and helmet in a bag, grabs his skateboard, takes the elevator down to his car and drives to the Skate Masters event in Venice. He parks a couple of blocks from the event, subtly disguised by a baseball cap and sunglasses, blending in with everyone else catching a glimpse of the opening action. A high energy buzz surrounds the ins and outs of the Skate Masters event. Skaters of all kinds stroll through in pleasant mobs. Stages of elaborate vert ramps and street courses occupy platforms over avenues along the Venice coastline. Elaborate tents for popular skate brands and food vendors firing up on the outskirts of the crowds create a festival atmosphere for the event. Rex rolls by slowly on his skateboard, swerving around the main path. He steps off his board to stare up at the big air ramp he'll be competing on. Finding his way through the crowds, following a trail of glimmering light between excited bodies, he notices a suspicious lingering huddle in an alley. The young cannabis CEO and two endorsers for Skate Masters exchange words with their eyes darting as they climb into a black SUV. Rex stands perplexed on his skateboard, watching them pull away then flinching at a grab on his hip. Twirling around, Rex finds the boy skating circles around him with a smile across his face.

The boy takes off through the crowd, looking back for Rex to chase after him. The sun soars high up in the pure blue sky as Rex ducks and weaves through the crowd, looking out to the calm ocean waves layered with glittering light. He catches up with the boy at the start of one of the street competitions. He leads the boy through the crowds to a roped off perimeter of the skating area. He tilts his disguise and security lets them both under the ropes. Rex brings the boy around to some of the other competitors, who give them an enthusiastic welcome as the run begins. They all stand watching with the best view of the final street competition for the day. Rex is swayed from the routine when he notices a line of flyers taped to the back of one of the ramps. He scopes one of the flyers and his heart skips a beat. Without processing the full clarity of the photo on the flyer, he can see there is a resemblance to the boy.

Rex steps forward in a trance. Walking on air, he moves in the path of the flailing line of flyers. His focus is startled by the leveling blow of a collision between himself and the skater performing his final routine. They're both tossed back, Rex losing his disguise. The astonished crowd yells, laughs, and murmurs in united upheaval. Rex is blitzed by security. Suddenly heeling at the sight of his identity, security guards help him up and escort him out of the way. Unhindered by the roaring voices competing for his attention, Rex escapes security's escort and runs towards the flyers. He rips one flyer off to see for sure that it's the same boy. He looks back to where they were just standing, but the boy is gone. Rex searches high and low for him, losing himself in the scurrying fans roaming the vast grounds of the event.

In the crowded back seat of a black SUV, Wheeler's tranquilized mind emerges back into a conscious state. His fluttering eyelids and saccadic eyeballs scan the air around him. Both of his security guards sitting up front, two Skate Masters endorsers in the middle row, and in the far back sitting next to him is the cannabis CEO with the snakeskin backpack. Wheeler puts his fingers up to his neck where the sedation dart penetrated his jugular. He rests as streaks of the city slide past him, his deteriorated muscles and altered state of mind hindering his ability to respond.

They stop at a closed restaurant along the coast. The security guards get out to remove duffle bags from the trunk behind Wheeler's knackered body. The young CEO pats the back of Wheeler's sandy head, flaunting a grin at him through the trunk as he mockingly shouts, "Go get 'em, hero!" He and his two associates, along with the two Skate Masters endorsers, exit the vehicle with unmarked duffle bags.

Wheeler stretches out in the back seat, all too quietly, being driven back to his beachfront property. He enters the echoing estate. Trudging up the winding staircase, he flings his bedroom door shut behind him, collapsing on his bed. Adjusting himself, he pulls his notebook out from underneath him. Flipping through pages, he pauses on a folded map stuck in the binding. The map is marked with dotted lines labeling Skate Masters secret locations in Hollywood, Santa Monica, and Venice, along with labels for scattered shops and restaurants running along the coast, with a big red "X" marking the Beverly Hills cannabis headquarters. Wheeler turns to the next page. Wiping sweat and blades of grass from his forehead, he flips the page again, revealing names and numbers relating to money laundering accounts in Switzerland, illegitimate skate sponsorships and shell cannabis companies running trade routes across Los Angeles. All of it, linking together a network with a sharp, powdery secret. Wheeler closes his notebook. Shuttering from queasiness, he rolls over on his side to get some shut eye, but the time on his alarm clock indicates a sobering reality. He faces Rex in one hour.

Rex runs back to his car and pushes on the ignition. Driving along the coast, he imagines the naked women sorting powder beneath the stairs of the cannabis headquarters, the two Skate Masters endorsers getting into the black SUV with the young cannabis CEO, the reality of facing off at a Skate Masters event put on by an organization he has refused to sign a new contract with, and the boy, lost and wandering between all efforts to find him. All of it plucking the strings of his orchestrated thoughts, placing him in all directions, leaving him staring at the red traffic light hovering above the line of cars sitting in front of him.

Rex lights half of a joint resting in his cupholder as he waits in the right lane by the entrance to a hospital. Music plays softly through the speakers as he puffs delicately, releasing smoke into the dispersing clouds above him. The light turns green, but nobody seems to move. His attention darts in front of him as he tries to make sense of a young woman with knotted, wiry hair, wearing only a hospital gown, pounding on the passenger side window of the car in front of him. Rex becomes motivated by her sudden departure from that car to his own convertible. He bursts to reach his arm across to lock the passenger door, but his seatbelt catches him tightly, locking him in place. The rogue woman flails her arms into the passenger side of Rex's convertible, attempting to unlock the door from the inside. Rex tosses her arms aside, trying to keep her out. She tumbles over the door headfirst, her entire body making it inside the car. Rex pushes her left shoulder up against the side of the passenger side door, his eyes searching for anyone around to take notice as the traffic surrounding them remains momentarily stationary. She wails and pleads for a ride. She begs Rex to take her to see her dog only a few blocks away. Rex cannot help but stare at her appearance. Her hospital gown flutters in the wind as she clings to a blood bag with IV tubing still in her arm. The cars around Rex begin to move. His thoughts freeze with no time before the event. He agrees to take her.

She sits with her legs curled up and eyes closed, soft tears falling down her cheeks. Rex drives on, intermittently glancing over at her. She nods off every few seconds before her looping head comes back around to see the world. Rex shudders at the raised needle marks running along her arms, scarring and bruising their way throughout her delicate veins, appearing like menacing beetles rummaging around with no regard for the tenderness of her skin. Rex arrives moments later at her destination. She opens an eye, requesting to go only a couple of blocks inland of the beach to a faded gas station up ahead. She looks back at Rex with eyes that seem delighted by the presence of malice and fear. She mumbles as they come to a stop, "Wanna do heroin?" Her words screeching on a chalk board, purring the twisted song of a junkie witch. She hunches her back, trotting away to the sidewalk lined by a colony of faded tents. She leaves Rex's passenger side door swung open as she finds a tent with two men standing calcified next to it, not batting an eye at her. She unzips the bottom, disappearing through a tear in reality. Rex gets out of the car, heart in his stomach, glancing at the men standing beside the tent, their souls itching beneath the skin. The haunting bumble bee hue surrounds their eyes, revealing diseased blood lurking through their vital organs. Rex hollowly shuts the passenger side door and pulls away. The image of her remains in his head all the way back to the Skate Masters event.

Wheeler, his band of family members and security guards, all get out of the black SUV in a parking garage at the Skate Masters event. Wheeler takes two steps toward a trash can and pukes just before leaning over the top of it. The two Skate Masters endorsers guide him through a hallway as Skate Masters event staff pass him his gear to suit up. Wheeler stumbles through the tunnel. Reaching the roped off crowds, he feels their vibrant energy. A red carpet is rolled out past the fans and camera crew, enabling a path to steps leading up the big air ramp. Wheeler hurries his stride, praying not to hurl again while waving to blurs of fans. He climbs the steps of the ramp with his security guards remaining on ground level. Two Skate Masters endorsers emerge at his sides from the top of the steps, quietly letting him know that given his current physical condition they will only allow for one run of the ramp each, believing this will give him the best chance at defeating Rex.

At the very top of the ramp, Wheeler looks out at the rippling effect of the crowd performing the wave along the curved stadium seats. He stares at his quivering hands, jolting his glance from muscle cramps, noticing there, next to him in the corner of the ramp's apex, with the sun exploding over his shoulders, is Rex staring back at him. Wheeler is about to crack a smile when the announcer blares over the whole event, "Ladies and gentlemen, let's give it up for Wheeler!" Wheeler lets his tongue slip out of his mouth, waving to the faces of the crowd. He slides his skateboard up to the edge with two wheels up, his shaking foot taps the board against the rail of the monstrous ramp. The feeling of freedom slips to one of doubt as he shifts his other foot to the tip of his skateboard. Weight tilting forward, he topples over the edge. Wheels racing and senses weightless, his control relies on muscle memory as he soars down the ramp. Accelerating past the flat surface, he hits the launching point. Sailing upward, twisting into a state of indecision, he loses sight of what's below. In a purgatory of hope, his mind flees from the idea of winning. The board disappears from his grasp as he contorts his body to fall smoothly, but without avail he falls awkwardly, slamming to the opposite end of the ramp with his shoulder, breaking his arm. Spitting out in pain, Wheeler tears up at the shock and agony of his broken limb. Embarrassed and done for, he is escorted by medical off the scene.

Rex squats down, holding his helmeted head in both hands. He stands scanning the crowd as the announcer murmurs over the loudspeaker. Rex looks out at the crowd, peering over a sea of people, when he unexpectedly locates the boy skating along a sidewalk outside the event. He scampers down the steps of the ramp, grabbing one of Wheeler's security guards to help direct him through the crowd. The confused and excited spectators watch him on the big screen as cameras follow them parting their way through the throng. He sprints outside the event ropes and, catching up with the slowly rolling boy, jumps in front of him. The bewildered boy looks around at the cameras swarming around them. Rex takes him by the arm, leading the way back to the big air ramp. The fans cheer and applaud as Wheeler's security guard accompanies them through.

From the depths of the crowd, the most beautiful young woman Rex has ever seen appears with a stack of flyers trembling in her hands. In joy and disbelief, she falls to her knees as the lost boy runs into her arms. She kisses him all over his messy head as his arms hug around her neck. The crowd jumps up and down, celebrating the joyous reunion as she reaches her hand out to grab Rex, mouthing "thank you," with ecstatic tears running down her face. The boy grabs her and Rex by the hand, tugging them up the steps, only to find the young man with the snakeskin backpack, two Skate Masters endorsers, and Wheeler in an arm sling, standing in their way. The young man gestures gratuitously for the boy to show the way up to the top.

Behind a curtain at the ramp's peak, where cameras hide behind the scenes, the young man steps forward to face Rex and says, "We need you to forfeit." He unveils a pistol in his waist as he goes on, "Wheeler is our winner." Pointing the gun at the boy and his mother he demands, "You two, move!" He brandishes the gun at them impatiently. The boy and his mother, innocent and afraid, stare at the loaded gun. She kneels down to her boy, placing his distraught face in her hands to communicate in sign language with him, "I promise you; it will be okay." The boy smiles faintly, replying to her in kind. The young man begins to yell at them both. Turning the gun on Rex, who is on his toes, teeming with desire to disarm him, but unable to react before Wheeler bolts suddenly, punting the gun out of the young man's hand, sending it flying into the curtain. Wheeler kicks him solidly in the chest. Rotating swiftly, he kicks him in the chest once more. Stumbling back, the young man is met by a final spinning kick to the face by Wheeler, sending him over the railing of the ramp. Falling far to the ground, he is caught in the arms Wheeler's security guard, who opens the back passenger side door to a black SUV, forcefully placing him into the interior of the car and following heftily behind before shutting the door.

Both Skate Masters endorsers hurriedly move down the steps to escape as Wheeler looks over at Rex, the boy and his mother, with a vivid smile. Rex smiles back at Wheeler, turning to the most beautiful woman he has ever seen as she stands close to her son, with a new set of eyes. Rex walks to the edge of the ramp. Peering down at the monstrous slope, he drops in. Before the announcer can utter a word, Rex ignites down the ramp. He imagines her with her boy as they stand watching him now in silent bliss. Rex booms up the launch ramp, body shooting skyward, leaving the past behind. Skateboard detaching from his grasp, he glides through the depths of a black and starry ocean, toward them both shimmering in suspended light, their guiding hands reaching out to him. Rex extends far out in front of him, his fingertips barely graze the rough edge of his skateboard. He opens his eyes to the whole world underneath him.

In a flash, Rex deftly pulls the skateboard out of clear day, placing it beneath his feet just before hitting the floor, landing the jump perfectly. The whole crowd erupts as he zips his way down the other side of the ramp, cutting to a sliding finish. He spins around with the face of a dream won, gazing up to the top of the ramp to see them both jubilantly embracing as Wheeler stands beside them, applauding his free hand to his heart.

Mother and son slide down the monstrous ramp and rise up into Rex's open arms. He kisses her passionately as the announcer stumbles to capture the essence of the moment. Wheeler walks down the steps into the celebration, microphones sprouting up in his face. He smiles broadly, staggering backwards as the crowd makes way for a descending helicopter. Hoisted up and carried above mobbing reporters by fans, Wheeler glides through the open helicopter door, his head falling into the lap of a female pilot with long dark hair and aviator sunglasses. Wheeler swings his arm sling around, kissing on her neck and slamming the helicopter door shut with his foot. They disappear into the burning sky. Rex gazes after the helicopter before turning to face a pair of starry eyes reflecting his vision. She kisses him deeply. Retreating from his face, she twists around to reach far out to the escaping hairs on her son's head. The boy throws his skateboard ahead, breaking out into the dawn of summer.

Acknowledgments

Rex vs. Wheeler would not be the same without the striking editing contribution from my father, Arnold. Thank you, Dad, for helping to change this book for the better. I will always appreciate the time we shared working on this book and everything else. Thank you to my mother, Eileen, for having faith in me on this journey and for her loving inspiration. Thanks to my sister, Shannon, for always having my back and for being the best big sister ever. Thank you with a bear hug to my grandparents for loving me all of my life and for encouraging me to do my best. Thanks to my friends and their families for genuine love and support always. Thank you, Zara Danyal, for your electrifying cover art. Thank you so much to anyone reading this now. I hope you enjoyed it. I love you all to the moon and stars. I will never forget my time spent creating *Rex vs. Wheeler*.